FOR SALE
FOR RENT

For Peter, Theo & Chewie the cat

THIS IS A BORZOI BOOK PUBLISHED BY ALFRED A. KNOPF

Library of Congress Cataloging-in-Publication Data is available upon request.

ISBN 978-1-9848-9336-9 (trade) — ISBN 978-1-9848-9337-6 (lib. bdg.) — ISBN 978-1-9848-9338-3 (ebook)

The illustrations in this book were created using watercolor, gouache, collage, and colored pencil.

MANUFACTURED IN CHINA

August 2020 10 9 8 7 6 5 4 3 2 1 First Edition

THE BLUE HOUSE

BY PHOEBE WAHL

Alfred A. Knopf New York

Leo lived with his dad
in an old blue house
next to a tall fir tree.

The paint was peeling,
and the roof was mossy.

There were leaks and creaks.

And when the wind blew,

the whole thing shook.

But it was theirs.

THE HOBBIT

Leo loved the blue house in winter, with its hiding places and cozy spaces.

When the old heater broke, they would bake a pie just to warm up the kitchen.

They would dance.

Leo loved the blue house in summer, with its garden full of raspberries and tomatoes.

He would play in the yard
until the sun went down.

Lately,
there was all kinds
of construction going on
in the neighborhood.
Big, new apartments were going up
next door and across the road.
Leo would watch the backhoes and trucks
out of his window.
They looked like tiny toys.

LEO

"I'm worried ours will be next...," he heard his dad say on the phone one night.
But Leo knew his dad was wrong.
The blue house would be theirs forever.

One day, Leo's dad picked him up from school. But instead of going home, they got ice cream and went to the beach. "I got a letter from the landlord today," Leo's dad said. "They've sold our house, and it's going to be torn down. I'm sorry, bud. We're going to have to move."

LEAVES
LEGA

Leo was angry. How could someone just take their house away?
He kicked and screamed and locked himself in his room.
They couldn't tear it down if he never came out.

But Leo got hungry and, after a while, went down for dinner.
"I'm angry, too," his dad said.

DADDY
So, after they ate, they danced and stomped and raged together. They shredded on guitar, and Leo did a special scream solo. It made both of them a little less mad.

Soon the blue house began to fill up with boxes. Every day another familiar object was packed away.

PLANTS
Books
Kitchen

When the blue house was empty, it was echoey and drafty like a hollow shell.
"The walls look so naked," said Leo.
"Let's paint on them," said his dad.

It made both of them
a little less sad.

The new house felt empty, too.
It didn't feel like home.

"I hate it," said Leo.
"That's okay," said his dad.

One day,
Leo and his dad
walked by the hole where
the blue house had been.

When they shut their eyes, they could see it clearly. Hear every floorboard's creak and the drip of the faucet's leak. But when they opened them again, their home was gone.

That night, as Leo lay in bed staring at the empty walls of his new room, he had an idea.

"What if we painted it?" Leo said.

"Good thinking!" said his dad. Then together, they mixed the perfect shade of blue.

And it made them both feel
a little more at home.

Little by little, familiar objects began to appear in the new house.

After school one day, Leo and his dad baked a pie in the kitchen.

OCTOBER
BLUE STAR
SUGAR

And that night, they unpacked
the stereo, and danced and
stomped and sang until it was
time for bed.

Leo had been right,
the blue house would be theirs forever.
And with each passing day, the new
house was becoming theirs, too.

2
3